Otto's Rainy Day

For Abrielle
Pamela R. Levy
10/20/01

Natasha Yim

Illustrated by
Pamela R. Levy

TALEWINDS
A Charlesbridge Imprint

*To my mom and dad, Margaret and Edward Yim,
whose love of literature laid the early foundations of
an interest in writing that ultimately made this book
possible. I owe them all my love and gratitude.*
—N. Y.

To my family, whom I love.
—P. R. L.

A *TALEWINDS* Book
Published by Charlesbridge Publishing
85 Main Street, Watertown, MA 02472
(617) 926-0329
www.charlesbridge.com

Library of Congress Cataloging-in-Publication Data
Yim, Natasha.
    Otto's rainy day/Natasha Yim; illustrations by Pamela R. Levy.
    p.   cm.
    "A Talewinds book."
    Summary: After several failed attempts to get Otto to play
quietly in the house, his mother finally gives in and goes
outside to play in the rain with him.
    ISBN 1-57091-400-1 (reinforced for library use)
[1. Behavior–Fiction. 2. Play–Fiction. 3. Mothers and sons–
Fiction. 4. Rain and rainfall–Fiction.] I. Levy, Pamela R., ill.
II. Title.
PZ7.Y5350t   2000
[E]–dc21   99-19695

Printed in the United States of America
(hc) 10 9 8 7 6 5 4 3 2 1

Illustrations done in watercolor on Winsor & Newton
watercolor paper
Display type and text type set in Caxton and Berkeley Old Style
Color separations by Eastern Rainbow, Derry, New Hampshire
Printed and bound by Worzalla Publishing Company,
Stevens Point, Wisconsin
Production supervision by Brian G. Walker
Designed by Diane M. Earley
Printed on recycled paper

It was a wet and rainy day.

Otto liked the rain. He liked listening to the sound of the raindrops.

He liked to run through
mud puddles.

He liked to splash little
ants on the pavement.

He liked to stick out his
tongue and taste the rain.

Otto put on his yellow raincoat. He put on his red rain boots.

"Where are you going?" asked his mother.

"I'm going out to play in the rain," said Otto.

Otto's mother shook her head.

"Otto, you have to play inside today. Mommy has some work to do for the office. I can't go outside with you, and I don't want you out there by yourself."

"I want to go outside and play," Otto declared crossly. He sat on the bottom stair with a big frown on his face.

"Otto," his mother replied,
"please don't sit there and pout.
You can't play outside in the
rain today. You'll have to find
something else to do."

Otto decided to slide down the banister.
He was a fireman sliding down the pole.
He had to put out a blazing fire!

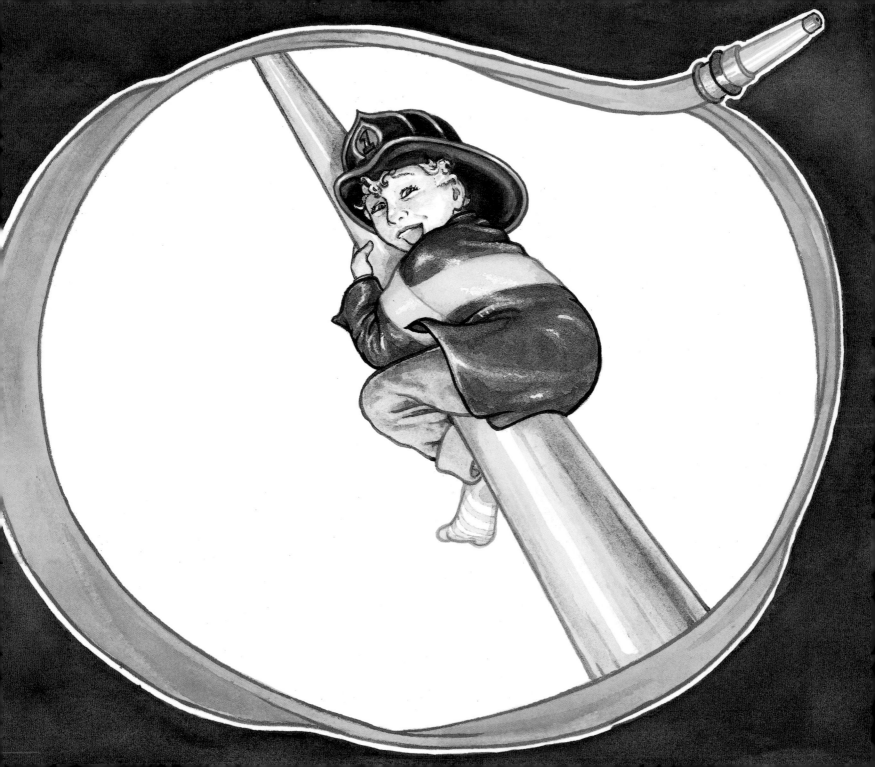

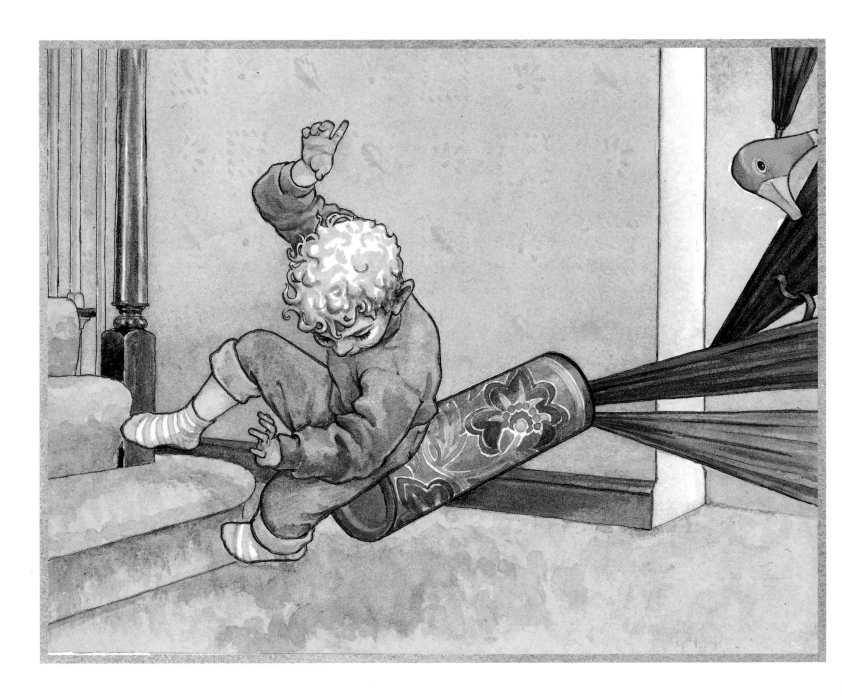

But Otto slid into the umbrella stand at the bottom of the stairs. The stand fell over, scattering umbrellas everywhere.

"Otto," his mother called from the next room, "don't slide down the banister. Pick up those umbrellas, and go play somewhere else."

Otto climbed up on his mother's new green curtains. He started to swing himself back and forth.

"Wheee! Look at me! I'm a monkey in a tree!" Otto yelled. He was in a jungle, swinging from vine to vine.

Bam! The curtains came crashing down, and Otto found himself on the floor with his feet in the air.

"Otto!" cried his mother. "Please stop making noise! Go play somewhere else."

Otto jumped onto the living room sofa. He jumped up on the arms. He jumped onto the cushions. He was a circus acrobat doing great stunts on a trampoline! Otto jumped higher and higher.

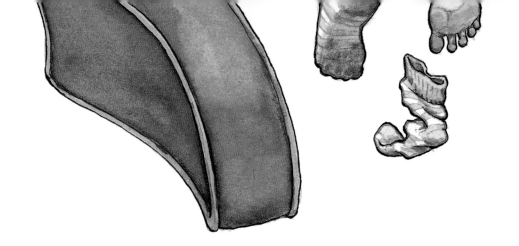

Suddenly, Otto bounced high up into the air. He landed on the seat of his pants on the floor. The cushions lay all around him. He had jumped too hard.

"Now what?" Otto's mother exclaimed in frustration. "Otto, for the last time, Mommy is trying to get some work done. Put the cushions back on the couch, and find something else to do before you break something or hurt yourself!"

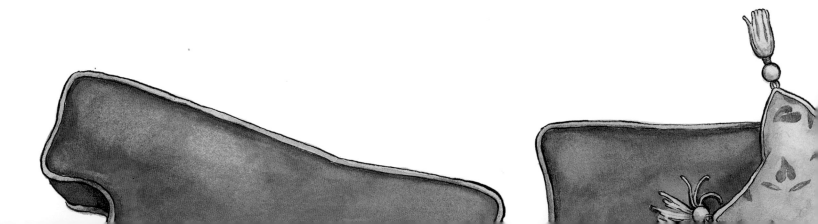

Otto went into the kitchen. He knew his mother was angry with him. He had crashed into the umbrella stand, pulled down the new green curtains, and messed up the sofa cushions.

"I know," Otto thought excitedly. "I'll bake a cake for Mommy. A great big chocolate cake! Mommy likes chocolate." Otto had seen his mother bake a cake many times before. "It didn't look that hard," he said to himself.

Otto was a famous chef with a big, white hat. He was baking the most mouthwatering, scrumptious cake in the world!

He put some eggs, sugar, and flour into a bowl and stirred everything together with a big wooden spoon.

Cake batter splattered on the table.

Cake batter splattered on the walls.

Cake batter splattered all over Otto's face.

There was now more cake batter outside the bowl than in it.

"Otto! Look at my kitchen! Can't you stay out of trouble?" his mother cried angrily when she saw what Otto had done.

"I . . . I was trying to bake you a chocolate cake, but . . ."
Otto said sadly, his lip quivering. "I'm sorry I made a mess
and made you mad at me." Otto began to cry. "I just wanted
to play in the rain."

Otto's mother sighed. She glanced at the dining room table where her papers were all spread out. She looked out the window at the raindrops falling on the grass and the trees. She looked at her son, who had tried to bake her a chocolate cake. Otto's mother gave one last look at her pile of papers.

Then she bent down and gave Otto a big hug.
"You know, honey, you're right. It's so much more fun
to play in the rain. Let's clean up the kitchen, and then . . .

. . . let's put on our yellow raincoats. Let's put on our red rain boots. And let's go outside and play in the rain."

Otto ran outside with his mother.
They ran through mud puddles.

They splashed little
ants on the pavement.

They stuck out their tongues
and tasted the rain.

Otto liked rainy days.